CORINNE V. DAVIES

RALPH IS (NOT) A VAMPIRE

ILLUSTRATED BY EL ASHFIELD

WHAT WICKED PEOPLE WROTE THIS BOOK?

Corinne V. Davies currently resides in the haunted and ghoul-ridden city of Edinburgh, where she continues to tour and run Ralph events, alongside writing about his latest misadventures. Possible vampire traits: extremely pale-skinned, very sharp canine teeth and a tendency to write books very late at night.

El Ashfield is the illustrator of this book and lives in the old, haunted town of Londinium (also known as London). She doesn't like garlic, or steaks (especially the wooden ones). El's current boyfriend is tall, dark, sleeps in a big odd shaped wooden container, has long pronged teeth and is very fond of cranberry juice...

For competitions, schools activity sheets and lesson guides or to join the Ralph fan club find us at: www.ralphisnotavampire.com or as Ralph the Superhero on facebook, Twitter us on @RalphSuperhero.

Publisher: RAL PUBLICATIONS, UK: a subdivision of Rocket-Mind Publications Limited. 5, Silverbirch Studios, Peebles, EH45 9BU United Kingdom

CHAPTERS

The next section is really scary, enter if you dare.
With quizzes, puzzles and schools activities in

"Solve the anagrams for each chapter and read a joke,
then hang upside down like a vampire to see the answers!"

CHAPTER 1
THE FANCY DRESS MESS

a) anagram: **FNOFIC**

b) joke: 'What is a vampire's favourite sport?'

Answers:
a) coffin   b) 'Bat-minton'

Young Ralph was not that popular –
His sister told him so
And if their paths should ever cross,
She'd always let him know
That he was just *'embarrassing'*,

whilst she was *'really cool'*:

'*Don't ever talk to me in public places*' was her rule.

Her birthday was approaching and her party had been planned,
The first vote was for fancy dress, but sadly this was banned
Because her friend, Prunella, said, 'a disco would be better!'
(Which gave Ralph's sis a chance to wear her new and

                                         sparkly sweater.)

Against her will, Ralph's parents had insisted he be there
(Though clearly if the truth was told, Ralph really didn't care)
And so his sister tried to get her own back…have a guess…
That's right! – She didn't tell him that it WASN'T fancy dress.

The party night arrived and poor Ralph's costume was complete
Outside he heard one hundred guests all pile into their street
Then head towards the big marquee his parents had erected
But if he'd glanced at their attire, he might have just detected...

His sister's evil plan, which was about to come to pass
In front of friends and family and all his sister's class.
As Ralph arrived, the music stopped, the conversation died
And Ralph, in vampire costume, stood completely mortified!

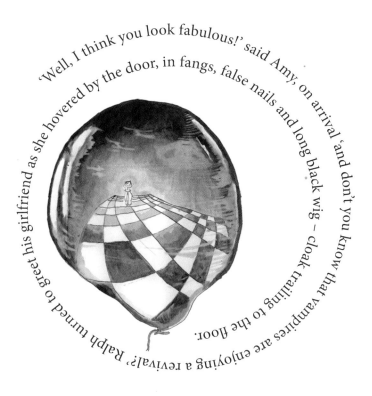

'Well, I think you look fabulous!' said Amy, on arrival 'and don't you know that vampires are enjoying a revival?' Ralph turned to greet his girlfriend as she hovered by the door, in fangs, false nails and long black wig – cloak trailing to the floor.

'Nice outfit!' smirked the football team –
Ralph felt his cheeks go red.
'But here's a tip, try wearing it for Halloween instead!'
"My sister told me it was fancy dress!" poor Ralph replied,
(A *shocking allegation* which big sis, of course, denied.)

10

'It's Mr. Vampire and his wife!' Prunella scoffed aloud
'You both look so ridiculous – you must feel really proud,
You've wasted all that effort dressing up and looking *weird*!'
As all his sister's classmates slowly gathered round and jeered.

"What makes you think that we're in fancy dress?"
                                             Ralph shouted out,
"We might be *real* vampires, there's a lot of them about!
You really shouldn't laugh at things you just don't understand,
Or I'll give your address to every vampire in the land!"

'He's not a *real* vampire…He's a joke!' Prunella mocked,
(Although she slept that night with doors and windows
                                             fully locked!)
Though Ralph and Amy tried their best to join in with the fun,
Each time they tried to socialise, the guests would turn and run.

'If you two feel uncomfortable…' Ralph's sis began to say
'…I'll try to phrase this nicely…you could simply GO AWAY!'
"That's fine…we'll go, dear sister – we could really not care less;
Myself and Amy would prefer a lovely game of chess."

So Ralph and Amy turned to leave with vampire heads held high
bewildering the older guests they quickly shuffled by.
Prunella shouted 'Night, night,
Mr. Vampire – what a joke!
You can't become a
vampire, just by
putting on a
cloak
!'

‘In

his defence…’

Ralph's friend began

‘I bet you didn't know

that Ralph has just one allergy,

that leaves his face a-glow.

He just can't stomach garlic –

so although he may be small…

It *might* be true that he's some kind of vampire after all.’

15

CHAPTER 2

THE SUNSCREEN SCANDAL

a) anagram: **LOWWFEER**

b) joke: 'How did the vampire keep his house smelling nice?'

Answers:

a) *werewolf* b) *'with an extractor fang!'*

The next day Ralph's big sister
Did admit to feeling bad
For forcing Ralph to leave
The greatest party that she'd had.

She really was surprised
That she was filled with such remorse,
But quickly recognised it would be
Temporary, of course!

'It sounds to me like what you feel is *guilt*.' Ralph's mum replied,
'Perhaps it's true, you love your brother *really*, deep inside.'
'I wouldn't go quite that far, but perhaps for just one day
I'll try to be quite nice and keep my rude remarks at bay.'

In fact, she took this further, as she had it in her mind
She must do something more,
that Ralph just might consider *kind*...
So broke into his bedroom and retrieved his dirty clothes
And thought she'd put a wash on

(knowing that's a job Ralph loathes!)

Ralph's Pad

19

However, in her haste, she didn't see the stray black sock
(Which clearly washed with all Ralph's whites was bound
to run a-mock!)
Despite her good intentions, poor Ralph's sister had conceded
That dyeing all his washing was the last thing Ralph
had needed.

"You really do seem sorry, sis," Ralph said with great surprise
"Let's face it, though, at household chores
you'll never win a prize.
Please NEVER do a wash again, you haven't got the knack,
As all the clothing that I own is now completely BLACK!"

And furthermore this didn't help his new found reputation
As someone giving vampires very serious contemplation,

For ever since the party, folk had given him wide-berth
As they were not entirely sure that Ralph was of this earth.

That weekend, Postman Speedy
Brought Ralph's chess-mag to his door
And mentioned his surprise
That he had not been told before…
That Ralph was now a fully paid up vampire –

                                  was it true?

And 'Should your fear of garlic
And black clothes have been a clue?'

"I'm not a real vampire, it's a rumour, that is all…
My sister dyed my clothes black and I'm only four feet tall.
I'm not a fan of garlic, I've an allergy, that's right –
But that alone does not make me a *creature of the night*!"

By midweek, back at school, however, things had worsened still
As Ralph had fuelled the rumour once again, against his will.
On such a sunny afternoon the teacher had suggested
Transferring to the school yard, as the classroom felt congested.

So Ralph had stopped en-route to put some sunscreen

on his nose
(His skin was rather pale and once he'd even burnt his toes!)
'What ARE you up to, Ralph?'

Prunella questioned, walking by…
And being Ralph, he didn't even contemplate a lie:

"Well since you ask, I'm really rather sensitive to sun,
So thanks for your concern, but now I simply have to run."
'It's true he *is* a vampire' said Prunella, in disgust.
'For everyone knows sunlight turns a vampire into dust!'

'We knew it!' said the football team. 'It's evidence indeed –
He's scared of sun and garlic…

how much more proof do we need?
That's why he loves the library, as he's sheltered from the glare
Of UV rays and sunlight when he's reading books in there!'

"It's getting out of hand…" Ralph said to Amy "…since last week
I've noticed all the kids at school, each time I go to speak
They glance away – as now they've heard the strangest

rumour yet…
That vampires can control your mind! (It's on the internet.)"

CHAPTER 3
DOWN SKITTLE

a) anagram: **TESEGNVARO**

b) joke: 'Why were the police after the vampire?'

Answers:

a) *gravestone* b) 'He robbed the bloodbank!'

So, naturally, Prunella used this further ammunition
To bully and torment poor Ralph – and set up a petition
To try to force the pupils to ensure their school would be:
Entirely *'Weirdo-Vigilant'* and always *'Vampire-Free'*.

The chess team just ignored Prunella and her wicked ways
As they were driven, focussed souls and very hard to faze.
Indeed, they pointed out that IF this vampire thing were true
Ralph could perfect his game at night – against a bat or two!

The papers soon ran articles on *'Local Vampire Boy'*
(Ralph's sis, of course, claimed it was an attention-seeking ploy)
And random neighbours tried to steal a little of his fame
By selling vampire stories (that were just a little lame!)

And yet, one friendly neighbour had refused to sell his story,
He really wasn't one for seeking money, fame or glory.
But still Prunella and Ralph's sis were quick to spread the word,
To everyone who'd listen and the few who hadn't heard…

That Mr. Ball, the neighbour, had a most intriguing pet
(This gave the Anti-Vampire club their biggest story yet!)
As Mr. Ball's pet, Skittle, was an energetic hound,
But every time Ralph glanced at him, he'd quickly go to ground.

Prunella shouted 'Never look a vampire in the eye!
For then they will control YOU, just like Skittle, which is why
We have to be prepared, as you see here what they can do:
Control the minds of werewolves and us *meeker* mortals too!'

"I think you'll find…" was Ralph's reply, "That Skittle hits the floor,
Because I give the 'DOWN' command –

that's clearly what it's for!
I went with Mr. Ball, last year, for one week's doggy training,
As Skittle had grown rather wild and neighbours were

complaining."

'He's lying!' said Prunella 'He's a vampire after all!'
'No, it's correct, Ralph helped me out, it's true!' said Mr. Ball.
'Now Skittle is a friend of Ralph's and frankly – what is more –
He's nothing like a werewolf…he's a golden labrador!'

Prunella scoffed and headed off, Ralph took another route.
He thought it over carefully and started to compute
That people like Prunella often felt the need to find
A shyer individual, to whom they were unkind.

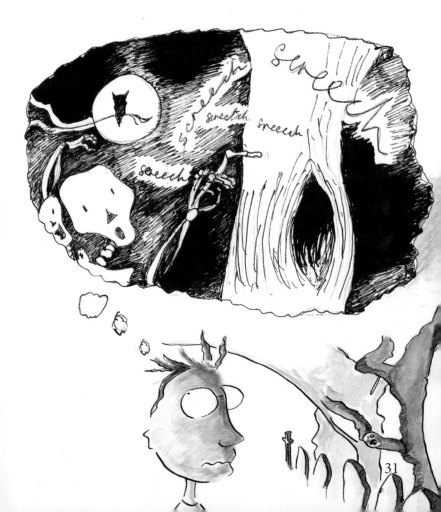

Ralph darted through the graveyard as the light began to fade,

Distracted by one gravestone he considered newly-laid,

But didn't check his footing, so his legs were in a knot...

And suddenly Ralph tumbled right into an empty plot!

wheeee

aaaaaaah!

RI

33

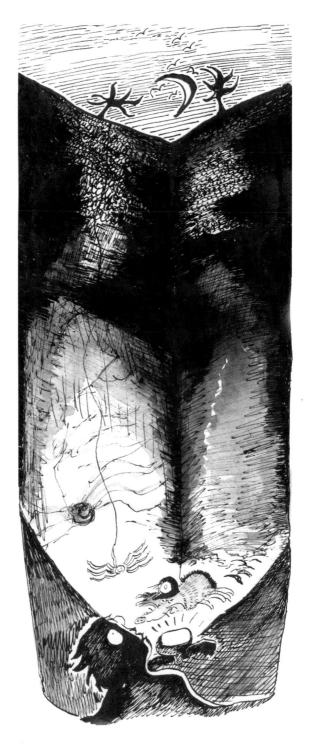

"Oh not again!" Ralph shouted out "Why is it ALWAYS me
These things just seem to happen to?...Now I'll be late for tea!
Plus mum and dad will worry (though my sis will worry less)
And by the time they find me I'll be such an *earthy* mess!"

Ralph checked his watch (which lit up in the dark) –

                                      two hours had passed.
His feet and legs were going numb – they had to find him fast!
Ralph felt assured by now that the police were on his case,
But would they think to look for him in such a random place?

Ralph heard some heavy panting and he hugged himself in fear,
For something big was out there and it sounded very near!
He closed his eyes and listened to the echoes in the dark
And quickly realised he could hear one familiar bark...

"Skittle?...Are you there?" Ralph boomed
"I'm here boy, in the ground!"
Ralph couldn't see a thing, but
Heard some voices gather round.
'Is that you, son?' a policeman
Said. 'Well, what a place to fall!'
And soon Ralph heard his mum
And dad, his sis and Mr. Ball.

35

Of course it didn't help his case –
The press arrived at speed.

> They saw Ralph pulled out from the grave
> And said 'That's all we need!'

The next day's papers helped
Ralph's reputation further slide

With '*Vampire Boy*
prefers to Sleep in Graveyards…
More inside!'

CHAPTER 4

BEWARE PRUNELLA...
OH AND CRANBERRY JUICE TOO

a) anagram: **CLROFEETNI**

b) joke: 'Who is a vampire's favourite superhero?'

Answers:

a) *reflection* b) *'Batman'*

A nd that same morning Ralph
Had found a note stuffed in his blazer
(Along with fruit bar wrappers,
Two felt pens and one eraser.)
It simply said

'BEWARE
PRUNELLA HAS YOU IN HER SIGHTS!...
SO IF YOU ARE A VAMPIRE
THEN I HOPE YOU'RE
ONE THAT BITES!'

"Oh dear," poor Ralph declared as he surveyed his current class
For someone looking guilty who just might have been the grass.
But as the lunch bell rang the girls and boys all fled at speed,
Their rumbling bellies hinting that they all required a feed.

Ralph sat down, next to Amy, as she sipped her cranberry juice
And whispered, "look at this...there's an INFORMANT

on the loose!"

But as she reached to take the note,

her drink flew through the air…

and left Ralph's school shirt covered –

red juice splattered everywhere.

'He's drinking BLOOD! He's drinking BLOOD!'

Prunella boomed aloud

As dinner ladies tried their best to stem the sudden crowd.

'It's only juice!' poor Amy cried 'It's JUICE and nothing more!'

(One dinner lady fainted on her newly polished floor!)

Ralph raced off to the toilets, though en-route he had concluded
that any thoughts it might wash off were clearly quite
deluded. But Lady Luck was nowhere near,
Ralph found himself soon greeting
the football team, who used
the loos to hold
their weekly
meeting.

'Hey Vampire Boy!' the Captain said. 'This doesn't look too good!
For if you claim you're NOT a vampire, then you really should
Take my advice – avoid red juice – tomato ketchup too,
If you want to convince us that this *vampire* thing's not true!'

"I'll bear all that in mind," said Ralph, then darted past in haste
And grabbed some soap and water and applied the frothy paste.
"It's just not coming off!" cried Ralph. "It's really such a shame…
And Amy will feel terrible as she's the one to blame."

Distracted by his shirt, Ralph didn't see the football team
All form a perfect line on either side of him , then beam…
Into the mirror, that was placed above the row of sinks
As Ralph just muttered, "sometimes all my bad luck

REALLY stinks!"

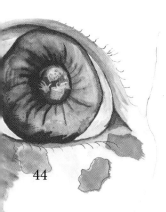

44

And then eleven voices chorused

out their football song

(Though Ralph tried hard to block it

out, he knew the tune was wrong!)

'WE'RE WINNERS!...

YES WE'RE WINNERS!'

they all chanted at the glass.

As Ralph just rolled his eyes and prayed

this moment would soon pass!

'Look Captain...' said one Striker

'...I'm not one to make a fuss

But by my calculations, well there should be

TWELVE of us.

Correct me if I'm wrong – but you will find on close inspection

That someone in this line-up's clearly missing a reflection!'

'He's right!' replied the Captain. 'There's eleven in our crew

And in the mirror I can see myself, plus ten of you!

But Ralph is stood here also – but his image can't be seen –

Remind me, what does having no reflection *often* mean?'

45

"I see where this is going, boys!" Ralph started to retort,
"The reason you can't see me in the mirror is – I'M SHORT!
Just bring a box, I'll stand on it – and then you're soon to see
Reflections of you all…and then an extra one of ME!"

'He's bound to say that, Captain!' said one Forward. 'What a lie!
You've no reflection, Ralph and we all know the reason why…
Because you are a VAMPIRE, not because you're rather small –
And blaming it on height…well, that just makes no sense at all!'

"Of course it does!" poor Ralph replied, but knew it was too late
As all the football team had fled – they simply couldn't wait,
To spread the latest word on Ralph and all his vampire ways
Whilst Ralph continued cleaning in a numb, bewildered daze.

"It's rotten luck…" Ralph muttered "It's becoming such a pain,
And now my only *un-black* shirt for school has got a stain.
I'll have to spend the afternoon avoiding the school nurse –
My only consolation is…things simply CAN'T get worse!"

CHAPTER 5
ANTI-WRINKLE CREAM FOR VAMPIRES

a) anagram: **KSDNSEAR**

b) joke: 'What did the vampire mummy give her son for his cold?'

Answers:

a) *darkness* b) '*coffin mixture'*

That Tuesday, early evening,
Ralph enjoyed a mug of tea
Whilst flicking 'Chess-Champs' magazine,
Where he was pleased to see,
A fascinating article on *'How to Move Your King'*
And so engrossed was Ralph, he didn't hear the doorbell ring.

Before he knew what hit him,
Poor Ralph's lounge had been invaded,
He glanced up from his magazine – his colour quickly faded,
Prunella (and supporters) lined up neatly in a row
Along with Ralph's big sis (and three or four he didn't know!)

"What now?" poor Ralph began
"Is it this vampire thing AGAIN?"
Prunella nodded silently, then clicked her ballpoint pen.
'We know about your secret and the *proof* is in my hand
And I'll make sure this reaches every corner of the land!'

"Go on…" said Ralph

"…I just can't wait, so what have I done now?"

'As if he didn't know!' Prunella scoffed with furrowed brow.

'We all know WHO YOU ARE Ralph,

Though I must say at this stage,

You're looking good for someone who's

FOUR HUNDRED years of age!'

'We know your real name's *'Ralph de Vamp'*

and you were born in France,
But lived all over Europe – Prague and Venice, at a glance,
Were born in 1650 – you were brought up by your nanny
And here's a portrait of you – the resemblance is *uncanny*!

"I've

heard of

Ralph de Vamp",

said Ralph,

"…A

giant,

bearded, man

who lurked amidst

the shadows as he

formed his evil plan.

His work was quite exhausting,

though – and so to lessen stress,

he'd fly back home and then unwind

by playing vampire chess.

They say that he used cannonballs to sharpen up his fangs
And terrified the members of the other vampire gangs.
But nobody dared marry him, which I think such a pity,
But would YOU marry someone who might polish off a city?

They say that he slept upside down, just hanging from the ceiling
-That he was bad at cooking (which all girls find unappealing!)
-Was brilliant at counting, which proves he was no-one's fool,
Although he bit 1000 men…I think he sounded cool!"

'Of course you would deny it!

        …That's what all you vampires DO!'

"So what did you expect?" cried Ralph

        "For me to say IT'S TRUE:

That I am *Ralph de Vamp* – the greatest vampire ever known?

You found me out!" poor Ralph replied (in slight sarcastic tone.)

55

'And furthermore…' she carried on, 'we've written down a list,
We think it's pretty thorough, but please add on what
we've missed.
We all looked on the internet for common vampire traits –
Their powers, personalities and common likes and hates:

- They frequently get headaches
  and they don't require much sleep.

- They often get flu symptoms,
  when their eyes and noses weep.

- They like to turn invisible
  and move with super speed.

- They have the strength of 20 men…
  what more proof do we need?'

"My headaches and flu symptoms are from allergies – no more.
I never move at speed for fear of ending on the floor.
So am I really *Ralph de Vamp*? Prunella, I agree…
At 6 foot 4 and super strong – sounds VERY much like me!"

Prunella and her team all fled, still mumbling, out the door,

Ralph shook his head and picked up 'Chess-Champs'

magazine once more. His sister told Ralph's

parents all this latest vampire news,

'400 years?' Ralph's mum replied,

'what night cream

does he

use

?'

CHAPTER 6

POPCORN FOR . . . ONE?

a) anagram: **ASFGN**

b) joke: 'Why did the vampire join a dating website?'

Answers:

a) fangs   b) He wanted to find a suitable ghoulfriend!

T hat night, however,
Ralph had brushed his teeth – quite unaware
A darkened mist was forming high above him
in the air.
Ralph put the toothpaste cap on, then he turned around to find
A giant vampire hanging from his bathroom roller blind.

'You summoned me?' said *Ralph de Vamp*
"…not really!" Ralph replied
'YOU DID!…and hence I've come to visit – from *the other side.*
I've walked the earth for all these years…I'll carry on until
I may amend my vampire ways, with one act of good will.'

"It's really you? You're *Ralph de Vamp*?…I'll go and fetch my sis,
She won't believe a word of it, if I don't show her this!"
'I'd love to help you out, Ralph, but my friend it's sadly true –
That I must be INVISIBLE to everyone, but you…

For only when a *worthy soul* has said my name aloud –
The *kindest* individual, who stands out from the crowd;
Yes, Ralph, you've been selected as the one to help me seek
My final peace and resting place – I'm giving you one week.'

"I've

got the very thing!"

cried Ralph, as he retired to bed,

Aware that Ralph de Vamp was hanging somewhere overhead.

"Four miles away is *'Tummy-Aid'* – a charity that makes

all empty bellies full, by giving

sandwiches and

cakes."

That

Saturday, both Ralphs

took off to offer their assistance,

they had to take the bus as it was really quite a distance.

Ralph asked his friend, "Do vampires need a ticket on the bus?"

'Remember I'm INVISIBLE – Ralph, please don't

make a fuss

!'

Upon arrival Ralph (and Ralph) could hear an angry din...
Apparently the night before some thieves had broken in:
'They've stolen ALL our tin-openers!' the chef cried in disgust,
'The only one they left behind is *blunt*...and plagued with rust!

You have to understand, Ralph, this has left us in a jam –
We've got no means of opening these FIFTY tins of spam.
The queue is getting longer, so I'm sure you'll understand,
We need a quick solution – or this might get out of hand.'

'Distract the staff' said *Ralph de Vamp*, then grabbed
the box of tins:
'I think I've found a way to be forgiven for my sins.'
Then, dangling from the fire escape – and far above the street
De Vamp had used his fangs to open FIFTY tins of meat.

The staff had asked no questions, they just served
the queue at pace
(And after all, they couldn't thank their hero 'face-to-face'.)

And *Ralph de Vamp* cried 'thank you,
Ralph – could anyone have guessed…
YOU'D be the one to help me to
my final place
of rest?'

Before the new friends parted, they took in a film or two –
It was the one thing Ralph de Vamp had always *longed* to do.
He loved the scary parts: the frightened screams

and sudden bangs,

But hated all the popcorn getting stuck within his fangs.

They hurried home, so Ralph could brush his fangs

before departing

(To make a good impression in this new life he was starting.)
He used the *whitening* toothpaste up, so big sis had complained...
But years of being a vampire – well, it leaves your fangs

quite stained!

'Goodbye young Ralph – and for your help,

I'd like to give you this...'

And hugged his new friend forcefully and gave his cheek a kiss.
You see...I didn't bite you! I'll be vegan from now on.'

And with a darkened mist, Ralph noticed

Ralph de Vamp was gone.

CHAPTER 7
THE GARLIC BREAD SWORD

a) anagram: **RRROSET**

b) joke: 'What is a vampire's favourite boat?'

Answers:

a) *terrors* b) *'Any type of blood vessel!'*

T hen after *De Vamp's* visit,
   Just as things were looking better –
   Old Postman Speedy brought poor Ralph
An URGENT headed letter,
From *'Scary Dreams Anonymous'* –
Who thought Ralph just the chap
To help their younger members
        who could
              barely take
                    a nap...

For fear, sweats and terrors – nasty visions in their head!
Ghouls and ghosts and vampires who would visit them in bed!

Creaks and bangs and voices in the middle of the night!
Anything that sprang to life, when they put out the light!

'We know that you are busy, Ralph, but could you spare two hours,
To tell our younger members all about your vampire powers?
To let them see you're normal and like reading books…and chess
And how you vampires are quite *nice*, but often get bad press!'

Ralph thought it over carefully and knew what he must do;
He couldn't turn his back on all these people that he knew
Were far too terrified to sleep, which was a tiring curse.
(Though Ralph hoped seeing him would help…and not just
make things worse!)

So Ralph arrived (in costume) and addressed the massive crowd
Of children (and some adults) who were there and not too proud
To all admit they'd come along, but had been rather wary,
As meeting *real-life* vampires, well it could be somewhat scary!

"I hope that this has helped..." said Ralph

                          "...And when you're scared, just phone,
Remember there is nothing we should *fear*, but *fear* alone!
There are no *scary* vampires, and so now you know it's true –
We're just a friendly bunch who might be just as scared of *you*!"

Returning
home, however,
Ralph was most upset to see
his sister had invited Miss Prunella
round for tea.
And just as
Ralph was thinking
nothing could be worse than that,
Ralph's mum was in their attic –
as she'd only found a bat!

"Well that's *terrific* timing!" muttered Ralph – Prunella beamed
'Is it your *pet*, you *vampire*?' then she turned around
and screamed.
The bat was heading for her, till she ducked and hit the floor

And fortunately the bat flew out the *(still ajar) front door!*

Naturally, Prunella was quite quick to spread the word
To anyone who'd listen and the few who hadn't heard…
That *'Ralph The Vampire'* now kept bats,
just flying round his roof,
Which surely was another piece of evidence, or proof!

Then, only two days later, Ralph's dad thought it might be nice
To lunch at 'Pizza Paradise' (you order by the slice.)
Ralph's sister had agreed to come, well...once it was agreed
She wasn't there to talk, just have a complimentary feed.

The waiter found an empty table for them – near the loos!
And Ralph picked up the menu and he started to peruse
The many different toppings and the ice-creams for desert
(Big sis complained her fork contained a tiny speck of dirt.)

'Not 'Vampire Boy' again!' Ralph heard the too-familiar tone
Of scheming, sly, Prunella, who by now was on the phone:
'Police! Police! The Vampire's here....Yes that IS what I said!'
(Whilst trying to keep our Ralph at bay, by waving garlic bread!)

"She's
got it in for me!"
poor Ralph told Amy, over chess,
"I just don't know what's left to try – it's such a *dreadful*
mess!"
'A few of us were talking, Ralph, we've come up with a plan –
and this is what you have to *do…*'
and so his friend began

…

CHAPTER 8

THE LIQUID LADDER

a) anagram: **RNNLCOUAT**

b) joke: 'What is a vampire's favourite yoghurt?'

Answers:

'You're not the only one, Ralph,
      To be bullied by Prunella.
      She once paid all the bigger boys
To lock Kurt in a cellar.
And next she was unkind to Claude –
And Katy's not that fond,
Prunella once deliberately
      pushed *her* into a pond!

So we all thought the time has come
to visit her one night

And try to stop her evil ways by giving her a fright.
I asked around the library – the chess team are on board,
Plus everyone she's ever crossed…like Katy, Kurt and Claude.

The
fool-proof
plan had been
devised, the date had
been decided. They all met
down the lane from where Prunella's
folks resided. And on the stroke of midnight,
they had formed a human ladder. (Ironically the middle
member had the weakest bladder!)

And Ralph, in vampire costume,
reached Prunella's window pane. 'Be quick, Ralph!' Amy
shouted, 'as it really looks like rain!' He tapped
the pane politely...'*Fling it open!*'
shouted Kurt. "They do that
in the films," said Ralph
"but I would

just get

hurt

"

.

'*Who's there?*' Prunella shouted from her quaking double bed.
Ralph squinted in the darkness and could just make out

her head,

"I hear that you have been unkind to many of my friends –
And so I'll give you just one chance to try to make amends!"

'He really sounds quite *scary*!' Amy whispered, full of glee
'Quick Ralph!' the middle member cried 'I *really* need a wee!'
'The only night…' Prunella squeaked 'I didn't turn the lock…
It's rotten luck a vampire was out flying round the block!'

"It isn't nice to mock folk who are *different*, or just shy,
So STOP IT NOW – or feel the wrath of all my friends and I!
You always reap just what you sow, Prunella – yes it's true -
If you think well of *others*, then they'll soon think well of *you*!"

'Now wind it up!…we're wet!'
said all the bottom members, straining.
'How come you're wet?' said Amy, 'as up here, it isn't raining!'
'I really tried to warn you all…' the middle member cried
'It just took far too long – I couldn't hold it in – I *tried*!'

The ladder then came tumbling down,

                with bottom members crying

And Ralph plunged from the window,

                (which Prunella saw as flying!)

She shook beneath her duvet, whilst the others fled to bed

With all Ralph's words of wisdom busy floating round her head.

And next day, back at school,

They saw Prunella's transformation,

For after Ralph had left she lay in frightened contemplation

Then reached the big conclusion when she got up in the morning

She wanted no more visits – so would heed the vampire's warning!

And in a bid to shake his vampire-image, Ralph conceded,
To buy some brand-new clothes, which (since they all turned black) he needed.
Some folk remained convinced Ralph still had
                                                  mind-controlling powers
So when good things would happen, then they'd always send
                                                  him flowers.

The police and local papers were, at first, a little vexed
These *'Vampire Revelations'* had them all a bit perplexed
But pretty soon the police were happy just to close the case.
The papers did one last report… (as they required the space!)

It seems to us that, either way, this boy is rather kind,
So even if he IS a vampire, do we really mind?
For even if they DO exist, we need not make a fuss…
For in Ralph's words, "they might be cool – and just as scared of us!"

- THE END -

THE VAMPIRE ZONE

Congratulations, you've dared to enter the vampire zone!

Start off by getting your fangs into this…Did you notice that the whole book was written in rhyme? Try reading it out loud and see if you can guess which rhyming word will be at the end of the next sentence. Did you guess right?

Ralph has started writing a vampire poem below, but lots of the words are missing. See if you can fill in the gaps and choose the rhyming words, or just write your own poem from scratch.

If I could be a vampire, I'd .... all (day/night)
Then I would .... (away/say) or (light/fright)
If I could be a vampire... (cool/scare)
And..(school/fool) or (dare/glare)

Written a good vampire poem? Why not e-mail it to Ralph (ralph@ralphisnotavampire.com) and see what Ralph thinks of your poetry skills!

Vampire-Art
Now time to get your fang-tip pens out and give yourself a fright......
Why not try to draw:

- **Your own vampire twin?** *(Draw a picture of yourself and then make yourself into a vampire like De Vamp! What is your vampire twin's name?)*
- **Your family dressed as vampires**. *(What would your sister / brother look like with big fang teeth?)*
- **Your teacher dressed as a vampire.** *(Does your teacher have big curly black eyebrows and long nails? Do they look better like this?)*
- **Why not draw some other scary monsters?** *(What about a zombie, a werewolf or a ghost? What colours would they be? Scary colours, like purple, red, slimy green? Draw their prickly or slimy or spotty skin! What are they wearing?)*

<u>Vampire Facts</u>

How well do you know your vampires? Which of these answers do you think is the correct one?

You can kill Vampires by:
- plunging a stake in their heart
- plunging some garlic in their nose
- making them eat a steak (with mustard)

Vampires come out at night because:
- they are trying to save electricity
- they forget to set their watches correctly
- they are allergic to sunlight

Vampires live for:
- ever
- a long time
- about as long as your nan

Vampires come from:
- Eastern Europe, Russia and Transylvania
- Mars
- The bottom of my garden

Vampires have very long teeth because:
- they like to help people chop down trees
- they don't have any scissors so they use their teeth
- they like to drink blood!

Vampires sleep:
- in sleeping bags (fluffy ones)
- in bunk beds (with zombies)
- in coffins

• plunging a stake in their heart • they are allergic to sunlight • ever • Eastern Europe, Russia and Transylvania • they like to drink blood! • in coffins

Ralph's glossary of hard words from the book

Just in case you found a few of the words in the book hard to understand, I thought I'd check with my sister what they meant. However, she was busy painting her toe-nails and watching television and I'm not entirely sure she was really listening, so I also looked up roughly what they meant in all my dictionaries too. See if you can tell which answer is which!

allegation
A: *I think you'll find it's a bit like a crocodile…but your spelling is all wrong!*
B: The suggestion that somebody has done something wrong.

conceded
A: *Is it when a bad 'con' man does some planting in your garden?*
B: Agreed something is true after all, when you weren't sure at first.

marquee
A: *A nickname for Mark Elliot on the football team?*
B: A large tent used for functions or parties.

mortified
A: *Well I don't even know what 'tified' is…so how do I know if I want MORE of it?*
B: Very embarrassed or ashamed.

perplexed
A: *Is it when you make something purple, even if it doesn't want to be?*
B: When you feel completely confused or puzzled.

quaking
A: *Oh please! That's easy. It's the noise that ducks make, but again, you really must learn how to spell!*
B: Shaking or trembling.

retort
A: *Is it a brand of clothing? I'm sure my friend, Sophia, has some jeans by 'Retort'. I think it's a new label.*
B: A reply in quick, angry or sometimes even funny, manner.

vegan
A: *Ummm, a V-shaped water pistol?*
B: Someone who doesn't want to eat or use animal products in any way.

All right answers are B.

The Great Vampire Wordsearch

See if you dare find the following words from the book hidden in the grid (they might be hidden upwards, downwards, backwards, forwards or even at an angle).

Ralph de Vamp   **cloak**   **Skittle**   **terrified**
Prunella   **sunlight**   **dark**   **bitten**
                    flight   **invisible**

s	a	n	w	t	b	t	k
g	j	f	c	g	o	e	a
a	l	l	e	n	u	r	p
m	s	i	l	e	j	r	d
f	p	y	t	p	n	i	m
b	r	a	t	b	e	f	h
l	e	w	i	x	h	i	v
e	c	b	k	l	p	e	g
l	z	i	s	f	m	d	t
b	g	t	u	d	a	r	k
i	d	t	c	f	v	a	g
s	s	e	k	i	e	z	i
i	a	n	p	k	d	o	l
v	j	t	r	o	h	s	f
n	q	u	e	z	p	y	h
i	d	h	x	s	l	c	w
b	m	f	k	g	a	b	e
c	i	t	r	l	r	u	t
k	a	o	l	c	v	l	i
s	u	n	l	i	g	h	t
n	f	a	j	b	m	d	j

Book Discussion Point/Activities for Schools:

- Do you think there is a moral to the book? If so, what is it? How does Prunella change her ways?
- How does the fact that it is written in rhyme make the book different?
- What is your favourite chapter and why? What is the funniest moment?
- Who is your favourite character in the book and why? Which character do you relate to the most?

Why not?…

- Pretend you are one of the reporters that saw Ralph 'rise from the grave' in chapter three. Why not write your own headline and article about the incident?
- Write you own story about your 24-hour adventure with your new vampire friend?

If you have enjoyed reading 'Ralph is (not) a Vampire' why not try 'Ralph is (not) a Superhero' also by Corinne V. Davies and El Ashfield? So, until we meet again on Ralph's next great adventure…
'May the power of Ralph be with you!'

THIS BOOK IS DEDICATED TO

our immensely talented (and mercifully very un-vampire-like) graphic designer, Klara Smith, whose skill and dedication to Ralph have made this book such a thrilling and vibrant read once again! Special thanks also goes to Frederique, Mike and all at University of the Arts, London, for the **Creative Seed Fund Award** and for all your support; to Mags & Glenda and the fab team at RAL; and to our favourite kids: to Oscar & Max from Aunty El, and to Honor and Calon. And a massive "ta!" to our Ralph fan base and to all those who e-mailed us their favourite vampire jokes, particularly those who couldn't quite remember them! *CD & EA.*